First published by Walker Books Ltd.
87 Vauxhall Walk, London SE11 5HJ

Based on the Audio Visual series "Maisy." A King Rollo Films production for
Universal Pictures International Visual Programming. Original script by Andrew Brenner.
Illustrated in the style of Lucy Cousins by King Rollo Films Ltd.

Maisy™. Maisy is a registered trademark of Walker Books Ltd., London.

First U.S. edition 2001

Library of Congress Cataloging-in-Publication Data is available.
Library of Congress Catalog Card Number 00-108514

ISBN 0-7636-1500-5 (hardcover).—ISBN 0-7636-1502-1 (paperback)

10 9

Printed in China

This book was typeset in Lucy Cousins.
The illustrations were done in gouache.

Candlewick Press
2067 Massachusetts Avenue
Cambridge, Massachusetts 02140

visit us at www.candlewick.com

Maisy at the Fair

Lucy Cousins

CANDLEWICK PRESS
CAMBRIDGE, MASSACHUSETTS

Maisy and Tallulah
are going to
the fair.

Look at all the
rides and treats!

First Maisy and Tallulah go on the big slide.

Wheeeeeeeeeee!

Then they
jump inside the
bouncy castle.

Boing, boing!

Maisy rides the merry-go-round.

Up and down.
Round and round.

But where is Tallulah?

Maisy can't find her anywhere.

Now Eddie's in the bouncy castle.

Boing, boing!

Have you seen Tallulah?

Yoo hoo!

There she is,
way up high.

Maisy and Eddie get on the Ferris wheel too.

Have fun, everybody!

Goodbye, Maisy!
See you soon!

Lucy Cousins is one of today's most acclaimed author-illustrators of children's books. Her unique titles instantly engage babies, toddlers, and preschoolers with their childlike simplicity and bright colors. And the winsome exploits of characters like Maisy reflect the adventures that young children have every day.

Lucy admits that illustration comes more easily to her than writing, which tends to work around the drawings. "I draw by heart," she says. "I think of what children would like by going back to my own childlike instincts." And what instincts! Lucy Cousins now has more than thirteen million books in print, from cloth and picture books to irresistible pull-the-tab and lift-the-flap books.